Pirate Bob

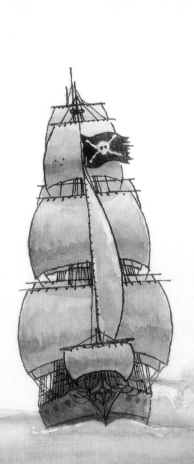

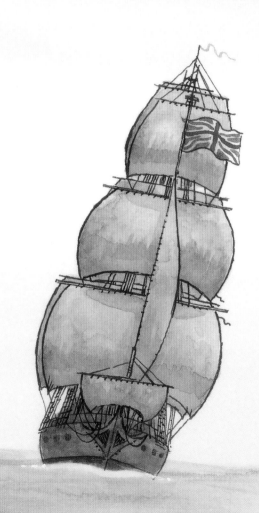

Kathryn Lasky Illustrated by David Clark

Charlesbridge

To Mary and Debbie of the Page Public Library:
My gratitude for your help with my research is
long overdue—D. C.

2008 First paperback edition
Text copyright © 2006 by Kathryn Lasky
Illustrations copyright © 2006 by David Clark

Published by Charlesbridge
85 Main Street
Watertown, MA 02472
(617) 926-0329
www.charlesbridge.com

Library of Congress Cataloging-in-Publication Data
Lasky, Kathryn.
    Pirate Bob / Kathryn Lasky ; illustrated by David Clark.
        p. cm.
    Summary: Describes the life of a pirate, named simply Bob, whose job is to
cut the steering cables and cripple the ships he and his shipmates will loot.
    ISBN 978-1-57091-595-6 (reinforced for library use)
    ISBN 978-1-57091-647-2 (softcover)
[1. Pirates—Fiction. 2. Sea stories.]   I. Clark, David (David Lynn), 1960– ill.
II. Title.
PZ7.L3274Pir 2006
[Fic]—dc22   2005019621

Printed in Singapore
(hc) 10 9 8 7 6 5 4 3
(sc) 10 9 8 7 6 5 4 3 2 1

Illustrations done in ink and watercolor on Arches Aquarella paper
Display type set in P22 Operina and P22 Mayflower;
    text type set in Ogre, designed by the Australian Type Foundry
Color separations by Chroma Graphics, Singapore
Printed and bound by Imago
Production supervision by Brian G. Walker
Designed by Susan Mallory Sherman

This is a pirate's nose.

It has a scar that runs from its tip to the pirate's ear.

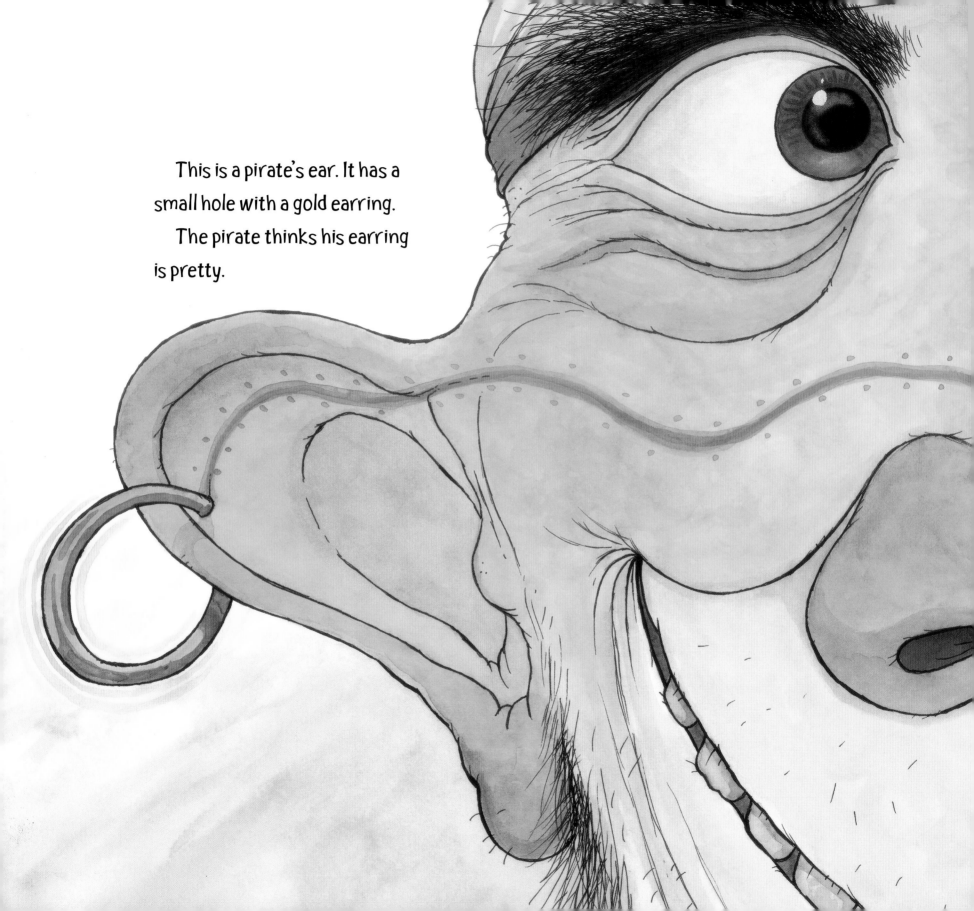

This is a pirate's ear. It has a small hole with a gold earring. The pirate thinks his earring is pretty.

Not all pirates have the same nose or wear gold earrings, but they all like gold and money and jewels a lot. They are so greedy for gold and treasure that they steal.

Sometimes Bob's nose itches, and sometimes it aches. When it itches, that means gold is near. When it aches, it is as if Bob's nose remembers the time when they raided the Spanish ship. The men had just stormed over the rail— flashing their cutlasses, their pistols spitting fire— when Bob ran right into the point of a cutlass. The wound left an ugly mark. It was after his nose was cut that Bob decided to wear an earring.

Right now Bob is waiting. And so are his mates on the ship *Blackbird*.
They are waiting for the perfect night and the perfect ship to plunder.
The favorite time of a pirate's day begins at night—a cloudy night with a
full moon, and on the sea a slow ship sailing heavy with gold or silver.

This is a rogue's moon. It is sometimes called a pirate's moon. It is bright enough to see by, but then the clouds scud across it, dimming the moon's light. This way the pirate ship can sneak up and attack.

Bob touches his nose.

"It itches, Jack," he whispers.

This is Bob's friend, Yellow Jack. Yellow Jack is called that because his skin is the color of a very pale lemon. Yellow Jack has scurvy. But Yellow Jack turned brighter than most.

"It's a good night, Bob," Yellow Jack says. "Light wind and a rogue's moon."

"Your face is brighter than that moon, Jack." Bob laughs. Jack snarls.

Just then the moon melts out from behind a racing cloud.

From the crow's nest, high in the mast, comes a bellow.

"Ship ahoy!"

Now all the pirates are alert. Their hearts beat faster. Their eyes begin to glint with dreams of gold as the captain comes on deck.

This is the captain. He is small. He is the shortest man on the ship. He has a pet parakeet. The parakeet's name is Elaine. No one knows why that is her name, but it is. No one knows why the *Blackbird* is the captain's ship, but it is, and it is he who commands the ship.

"Crack on sail!" barks the captain. "Loose the mainsail! Loose the topsail! Sheet home!"
These are all the commands for setting the square sails of the pirate ship. Bob and Jack
scramble up the rigging to untie the sails. They work side by side on the yards that fit across
the mast and hold the sails. Bob and Jack work well together. Jack hums.

"Don't worry, Bobby," Jack says in a kindly voice as they work. He can tell that Bob's nose
is hurting. "Think about the gold!"

Jack is a good friend, Bob's best friend. But having a best friend on a pirate ship can be complicated. Nobody trusts anybody. Yellow Jack has been a pirate for a long time. He has a lot of loot that he has buried some place. No one is quite sure where. He has a map that marks the spot, but no one knows where he has hidden it.

Yellow Jack likes Bob but thinks that Bob might like him only for his loot and might want to find out where the map is.

Bob genuinely likes Yellow Jack. He likes his jokes. He likes his stories. He even likes Yellow Jack's singing. But he wonders how much yellower Yellow Jack will get before he dies. And if he does die, it would be a shame for all that loot to lie buried forever.

The pirates sail closer to the ship, a galleon. Bob and Jack now stand by a cannon and await the captain's orders. They will shoot one shot over the bow. The captain does not want to sink the ship, for with it would go all the cargo and treasure.

Now not only does Bob's nose itch, but his fingers itch to light the fuse that will shoot off the cannon. All the pirates' fingers itch.

"Wait! Wait! Not too soon, lads." The captain's voice never wavers. The pirates know that he is counting to one hundred fifty, when they will be in range of the enemy ship.

By one hundred twenty they are close enough to see the name of the ship, but Bob can't read.

"*Concordia*," whispers Yellow Jack.

"Ccc . . . C . . ." Bob tries sounding out the name painted on the ship. The count goes on.

"One hundred forty-eight, one hundred forty-nine," Bob and
Jack count together under their breath.

"Fire!" shouts the captain. "Ready with the grappling hooks!"

Bob races for a grappling hook. He can hear the captain's voice.
The captain never seems frightened. His voice is still cool and
steady and clear.

"Avast! *Heave to, Concordia!* We'll blow you to kingdom come if you don't let us board."

The word "kingdom" is the signal. The grappling hooks are thrown. Their sharp points catch in the ship's rails, and then the pirates begin pulling the lines, hauling the English ship closer and closer.

"Right-oh!" That is the captain's code word for "board the enemy."
Elaine seems excited, too. She flutters her wings and tweets.

Bob forgets the ache in his nose. He has one thought, one purpose:
to cut the steering cables. And to cut anything, anyone, between him and
the steering cables that lead from the wheel to the rudder.

This will cripple the ship. This will earn Bob his share of the treasure.

Pirate Bob is an expert in wrecking wheels and rudders. He is fast. He is exact with his cutlass. He leaps over the rails. Others swarm aboard with him.

They carry daggers, pistols, and hand grenades made by filling old bottles with gunpowder.

Tonight Bob is lucky. The way to the steering cables is clear because the English sailors are busy trying to fire their cannon. The cannon will not work. Bob knows this because Yellow Jack is an expert at plugging the torch holes of cannons.

Each pirate has his job. The point is to get the cargo.
As Bob cuts the last cable, all is suddenly quiet.
He knows what this means.

  "Hand over!" It is the cool voice of the pirate captain.
The captain of the galleon surrenders.

The pirates are lucky. There is a lot of treasure. It takes them almost three hours to unload it. The ship has trunk after trunk of specie, gold and silver coins that it was carrying to the colonies in America in order to buy tobacco.

All the treasure stolen from the ship will be divided among the pirates. The captain and his first mate will get the most. The longer someone has been a pirate, the more he can expect. Bob will get a large share, since he has worked a long time on this ship. Yellow Jack has worked even longer and will get more.

That night there is a celebration. The crew is happy with all the loot.
Bob thinks he should feel happier. He has lots of loot now, but not as much
as Yellow Jack. While he slurps his soup and chews a chunk of turtle,
Bob tries to think of ways to ask Yellow Jack politely about his map and
treasure. But he is afraid that he will lose a friend. This is a true dilemma.

Bob thinks that he will keep on pirating for a few more years and get enough treasure of his own to bury someplace. He hopes that this will happen soon because being a pirate is dangerous work. You can almost get your nose cut off or lose a leg, like Peggy the Spanish pirate, or you can start to turn yellow like Yellow Jack. And even if none of that happens, you might be hunted down, captured, and hanged—for after all, pirates are outlaws.

Just one more ship, Bob thinks. One more Spanish galleon out of Havana, Cartagena, or Porto Bello. A few pounds of pearls, three or four of silver, twenty of gold, maybe a few emeralds. Then, he thinks, I'll bury my treasure and go out and look for friends—real friends who will like me not because they think I have buried treasure but because of who I am— plain old Bob with a scar on my nose and a ring in my ear.

Then, Bob tells himself, I'll be happy . . .

. . . I think.